Dear Parents,

Welcome to the Scholastic Reader series. We have taken over 80 years of experience with teachers, parents, and children and put it into a program that is designed to match your child's interests and skills.

Level 1—Short sentences and stories made up of words kids can sound out using their phonics skills and words that are important to remember.

Level 2—Longer sentences and stories with words kids need to know and new "big" words that they will want to know.

Level 3—From sentences to paragraphs to longer stories, these books have large "chunks" of texts and are made up of a rich vocabulary.

Level 4—First chapter books with more words and fewer pictures.

It is important that children learn to read well enough to succeed in school and beyond. Here are ideas for reading this book with your child:

- Look at the book together. Encourage your child to read the title and make a prediction about the story.
- Read the book together. Encourage your child to sound out words when appropriate. When your child struggles, you can help by providing the word.
- Encourage your child to retell the story. This is a great way to check for comprehension.
- Have your child take the fluency test on the last page to check progress.

Scholastic Readers are designed to support your child's efforts to learn how to read at every age and every stage. Enjoy helping your child learn to read and love to read.

> **—Francie Alexander**
> Chief Education Officer
> Scholastic Education

Text copyright © 1993 by Rita Golden Gelman.
Illustrations copyright © 1993 by Mort Gerberg.
Activities copyright © 2003 Scholastic Inc.
All rights reserved. Published by Scholastic Inc. SCHOLASTIC,
CARTWHEEL BOOKS, and associated logos are trademarks
and/or registered trademarks of Scholastic Inc.

Library of Congress Cataloging-in-Publication Data is available.

ISBN 0-590-45783-7

22 21   9 10 11 12/0

Printed in the U.S.A.   23
First printing, January 1993

More Spaghetti, I Say!

by Rita Golden Gelman • Illustrated by Mort Gerberg

Scholastic Reader — Level 2

SCHOLASTIC INC.

New York   Toronto   London   Auckland   Sydney
Mexico City   New Delhi   Hong Kong   Buenos Aires

"Play with me, Minnie.
Play with me, please.

We can stand on our heads.
We can hang by our knees."

"Oh, no.
I can't play.
I can't play with you, Freddy

Not now.
Can't you see?
I am eating spaghetti."

"Now you can do it.
Now you can play.

We can jump on the bed
for the rest of the day."

"No. I can **not**.
I can **not** jump and play.
Can't you see?
I need more.

More spaghetti, I say!

I love it.
I love it.
I love it.
I do.

I love it so much!"

"More than me?"

"More than you.

I love it on pancakes
with ice cream and ham.
With pickles and cookies,
bananas and jam.

I love it with mustard
and marshmallow stuff.
I eat it all day.
I just can't get enough.

I eat it on trucks,
and I eat it in trees."

"You eat it too much.
Won't you play with me,
PLEASE?"

"I can run in spaghetti.

And ride in spaghetti.

I can jump.
I can slide.
I can hide
in spaghetti.

I can skate on spaghetti,
and ski on spaghetti.

And look at this picture.
That's me on spaghetti."

"Spaghetti. Spaghetti. That's all you can say. I am going to throw your spaghetti away.

I am going to throw it
all over the bed,
in the air,
on your chair,
on the floor,
ON YOUR HEAD!

Oh, Minnie,
that look on your face!
You look bad.
You look big.
You look green.
You look sick.
You look sad."

"You are right.
I am green.
I feel sick.
Yes, I do.
I think I will rest.
I will sit here with you."

"Let me take this away now.
I think that I should.

And then we can play.

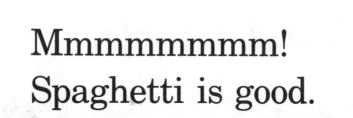

Mmmmmmmm!
Spaghetti is good.

I love it.
I love it.
I love it.
I do.
I need more spaghetti.
I can't play with you."

"But **now** I can play.
I can play with you, Freddy."

"Not now.
Can't you see?

I am eating spaghetti."